A DEADLY CALM

Anakin sensed Tahiri's presence. He raised his face and peered into the darkness. Slowly he rose to his knees, then gained his feet. Tahiri stepped out of the shadows and moved to Anakin's side. The side of his academy jumpsuit was drenched in blood, and Tahiri stifled a cry. Anakin grasped her hand tightly, and for a brief moment their eyes met. The look they exchanged was one of calm and resolve. They would fight the dragon together. . . .

STAR WARS

Junior Jedi Knights

Promises

Nancy Richardson

BOULEVARD BOOKS, NEW YORK

STAR WARS: JUNIOR JEDI KNIGHTS
PROMISES

A Boulevard Book / published by arrangement with
Lucasfilm Ltd.

PRINTING HISTORY
Boulevard edition / April 1996

All rights reserved.
®, ™ & Copyright © 1996 by Lucasfilm Ltd. Used under
authorization.
Cover illustration by Eric J.W. Lee.

This book may not be reproduced in whole
or in part, by mimeograph or any other means,
without permission. For information address:
The Berkley Publishing Group, 200 Madison Avenue,
New York, New York 10016.

The Putnam Berkley World Wide Web site address is
http://www.berkley.com

ISBN: 1-57297-097-9

BOULEVARD
Boulevard Books are published by The Berkley Publishing Group,
200 Madison Avenue, New York, New York 10016.
BOULEVARD and the "B" design
are trademarks belonging to The Berkley Publishing Group.

PRINTED IN THE UNITED STATES OF AMERICA

10 9 8 7

For
Forever's Children,

Scott Horsley
and
Parker Tomczak

Promises

PROLOGUE

There had been only one other day in Sliven's life when he could remember being afraid. It was the day he had fought his tribe to save the girl's life. The Tusken Raiders of Tatooine had been enraged that their leader, the fierce Sliven, would risk his own life to protect a human child.

It was not their way, Sliven's way, they'd growled and snarled. The Raiders were a violent, aggressive race that inhabited the sweltering deserts of Tatooine. They were nomads, roaming the desert wrapped head to toe in strips of white cloth, breathing through masks, and wearing heavy goggles to ward off the sand that whipped across their barren land. And when they needed precious water and food sometimes they stole it. Through stealth, or through violence. It didn't matter to them. Survival was their only rule. The tribe's survival.

1

They would not have searched for Sliven after the battle with a band of smugglers if he had not been their leader. Even then, they only searched for him because they couldn't name a new leader if the old one still lived. They had to be certain of his death. This Sliven knew, just as he knew how to travel through sandstorms, where the krayt dragons roamed, and the scent of a womp rat. They had come to find him dead, but he was alive.

Sliven watched the fiery twin suns of Tatooine slide behind the Jundland Wastes. He'd spent his life in this hot canyon and mesa region. A life filled with yellow sand, struggle, survival at all costs. Maybe if he hadn't known the girl's parents. If he hadn't come to them with the last of his life slipping from his body, been nursed back to health, lived in their home, ate with their small family of three. But it had happened, and it had changed him. And the result? He was still the same fierce Raider in appearance, but there was a part inside of him, a soft place, the place where his feelings for the girl lived.

The others had wanted to leave her there. To leave her to die in the empty moisture farm. It was at that moment, when Sliven had recognized that he would fight with his life to save the child, that he felt fear. The idea of dying for another being, not even one of his own race, a human infant, was strange to him. He had not expected the blonde-headed snip of life that giggled and smiled at his savage image to affect him more than the buzzing of black flies over the carcass of a bantha. But it had; she had.

And so he'd made a bargain. A promise that involved both her life and his own, and that would not be made known to the girl until the time came. If it went unfulfilled, Sliven would be killed. If the girl chose to do what needed to be done, she would be rewarded with the story of her family. A history that had been kept from her by the Raiders as part of the bargain. Sliven knew she might agree to try just to learn her history. But if she failed, she would die, and so would he.

The years have passed in the sigh of a bantha, Sliven thought. The child had been taken into the tribe, taught to hunt and fight, and to survive in the desert. He'd taught her those things, masking his concern behind the grunts and growls of his language. A language he'd taught her when she was only three years old, along with Basic, which he'd learned during his stay with her parents.

She might survive, Sliven thought. Still, part of him hoped that she wouldn't return to Tatooine. That she would stay with the Jedi who had discovered and taken her from the tribe to study at the Jedi academy on Yavin 4. She was strong in the Force, they'd explained to him. They wanted to train her to become a Jedi Knight. Sliven had agreed, for two reasons. First, he understood all too well what the leader of the Jedi, Master Luke

Skywalker, and the Jedi Knight, Tionne, recognized. After all, he'd spent several months with the girl's parents. They, too, had a strange power within them, and unusual abilities. Second, Sliven knew that the girl had to spend time away from the tribe, see other beings and places, in order to decide whether she wanted to spend the rest of her life as a Tusken Raider. To decide whether or not she belonged.

Sliven knew that the promise he had made years earlier had to be denied or fulfilled soon, so he'd made a deal with the child. The girl could go to Yavin 4 if she returned to her tribe in six months. He'd explained to the Jedi Master that in half a year Tahiri had to make a decision as to whether to return to her tribe or to stay on at the academy. If she chose to stay at the academy, she would forever lose the tribe. And she had to come back to her home planet, Tatooine, to say what she decided. Skywalker understood, and the girl had agreed.

But would she come? And if she did, would she choose to fulfill the promise? Sliven wasn't certain. He grunted deeply and sat unmoving in the stillness of the desert night. If he had loved the girl when she was only an infant, what he felt now threatened to tear his battered heart apart beneath its covering of ragged cloth. *I want her to remain with the tribe, to watch her grow up as I grow old. But I don't know if she belongs with us,* with me. And I want to live, Sliven thought in frustration, for I'm still strong enough, violent enough, to lead my people.

Sliven looked up to the night sky, to the stars which would guide her back to him. "Do not come back, my daughter," he called softly. "Do not come home, Tahiri."

 **ONE**

The figure loomed above him. Anakin tried to shield his eyes from the brilliant glare of the golden globe. Tried to see the being whose body was outlined with a shimmering blue line.

"Young Anakin Solo," a voice whispered, a hand beckoned. Anakin followed the glow of the being away from the globe. As he walked, he felt darkness pulling at the loose cloth of his orange jumpsuit. Fear fluttered in his belly, but he followed, using the Force to calm the racing of his heart. The figure stopped before carvings in the crumbling stone walls of the ancient Massassi Palace of the Woolamander. The hand flickered with pale blue sparks as it swept over the message.

Anakin's eyes scanned the symbols. He and Tahiri had finally been able to read them after returning from Yavin 8. Anakin read their message out loud. "Peace to all. We are the Massassi.

7

Our children have been imprisoned by the evil Jedi Knight Exar Kun. Locked deep within this palace, hidden in the glittering sands of a golden globe, they await. The crystal that holds them prisoner can only be unlocked by children, strong in the Force and dedicated to the battle of good over evil. If you are the ones, enter the globe and lead our children to freedom." The figure nodded, then fell to its knees before Anakin, head dropped. Anakin sensed its torment.

"Tahiri and I are the ones," he heard himself say. "Don't be afraid—we'll fight this battle." The pale blue line around the figure began to spark and flicker until it faded into the darkness. The being still knelt before Anakin, unmoving. Anakin bent down and reached out his hand. The figure slowly lifted its black hooded head and let out a roar filled with hatred and darkness. Anakin leapt away as it began to laugh in rolls of icy thunder.

Eyes the color of blue gray burning coals fixed upon Anakin, held him with their power. The figure rose, unfolding into a creature twice its original size. It continued to laugh, and Anakin felt swallowed by the darkness of its hollow cries. He ran, not knowing which way he traveled in the cavity of the palace. The black-robed being followed, howling in mad glee. Anakin reached the secret room that housed the golden globe he and

Tahiri had discovered months earlier. They had instantly sensed its evil, and pledged to understand, unlock, and free the prisoners that cried from its core.

His back to the globe, Anakin watched as the black-robed figure approached, once again fixing him with those burning eyes. He backed up until he couldn't move any farther without touching the globe. There was a powerful field around the crystal sphere. Tahiri had tried to touch it and had been thrown against the stone walls of the room. Anakin wasn't going to make the same mistake. He held his ground.

"I'm going to fight you," Anakin shouted. "Tahiri and I will use the Force to break the evil curse. We're the ones the Massassi wrote about: 'strong in the Force and dedicated to the battle of good over evil'! You can't stop us—"

"Why would I want to stop you, boy?" the figure laughed. "I am you!" The creature threw back its hood, and Anakin stifled a scream that welled up from the very core of his being and threatened to escape his trembling lips. He stood looking at his own face. Only his eyes were different. Instead of being a pure ice blue, they had been replaced with burning gray coals that smoked and sparked.

"Didn't you hear me, boy?" the figure snarled. "I'm you, you fool. You knew, you've always known that you were meant to serve the dark side

—to use the Force for evil. It's in your blood. Your grandfather served us well, helped us defeat the Jedi Knights. You were named after him, after Anakin Skywalker who became Darth Vader. Stop fighting us and embrace the dark side. . . ."

"It won't work," Anakin said calmly, summoning up the Force to control himself. "I know who you are." The figure hissed, recoiling from the power in Anakin's voice. "You're a follower of Exar Kun, the evil Jedi Knight who enslaved the Massassi race thousands of years ago by imprisoning its children in the golden globe. You're not me, and you never will be," Anakin went on, walking toward the robed figure. "Tahiri and I are going to fight you, and break the curse of the golden globe."

"This is not over, young Anakin Solo," the figure said angrily. Then its form began to waver in the golden light of the globe. Moments later, it had completely disappeared.

Anakin turned back toward the globe. He listened to the cries of the children from inside its swirling sands. Soon, he thought. Soon Tahiri and I will come to this place and attempt to enter the globe and lead you to freedom. "Soon, soon, soon . . ."

"Soon what?" Tahiri asked as she shook her best friend awake. "Anakin, wake up, you've been dreaming."

Anakin stared groggily up at Tahiri. Her green eyes were impatient, and he struggled to sit up. "What time is it?" he asked.

"Time for us to have a serious talk," Tahiri replied. "We've got a problem. I've been called to see Master Luke Skywalker. And I know why. I've been at the Jedi academy for six months, and it's time for me to make my decision about whether or not to return to my tribe or remain here."

"I thought you'd already decided to stay," Anakin said. Not only was Tahiri his best friend, but they were a team. A team pledged to solve the riddle of the globe.

"I have," Tahiri replied. "But it's not that simple. Master Luke and I agreed with Sliven, the leader of my tribe, that I'd return to Tatooine to make my decision. I've got to figure out a way to persuade Master Luke not to make me return. Right?" Tahiri didn't wait for a reply. "I mean, we've finally translated the ancient symbols in the Palace of the Woolamander. It's time to enter the globe—I can't go to Tatooine now! Aren't you going to say something?" Tahiri asked.

"I was just waiting for you to run out of breath," Anakin explained. He swept his long brown bangs out of his eyes and met Tahiri's questioning look. "I don't think it's going to be as easy as you think," he offered. "If you gave your word, and Uncle Luke did too, he's going to want you to return to Tatooine."

"I'll take care of it," Tahiri said. "Don't worry, I'm not going anywhere." With that, she strode out of the room to meet Luke Skywalker in the Grand Audience Chamber.

Anakin felt a sense of unease as his friend left. His dream had left him feeling anxious. The idea that someone might know about him and Tahiri, and their plans to enter the globe, hadn't occurred to him before. If Kun's evil followers knew about them, it would mean that the battle in the depths of the Palace of the Woolamander would be all the more difficult. He thought about that first time he and Tahiri had found the palace. They'd snuck out of the academy and rafted the river. A storm had forced them to abandon their raft and seek shelter. They'd found the palace, its strange carvings, and then a hidden spiral stairway that led deep into the crumbling site. As they'd descended, evil had coated the stones like thick black fungi, and dark whispers and threats had streamed through the dank air. And then they'd seen golden glitter, speckled along the walls and seeping from behind a secret doorway.

Anakin shook off the memory. Tahiri's right, I've got to stop daydreaming and focus on what's happening now. Anakin hoped that Tahiri would be able to persuade Uncle Luke to let her remain on Yavin 4 while making her decision. The time had come to break the curse. A moment of worry

reached out with fluttering yellow fingers and
touched Anakin's mind.

We are the ones, he thought. But are we strong
enough to enter the globe?

 **TWO**

Luke Skywalker studied the look of defiance. Green eyes flashed, and white blonde hair surrounded a stubborn nine-year-old face. Luke's blue eyes didn't falter as he waited for the child to speak. It would not be long. Tahiri was rarely lost for words. Luke thought about the time she and his nephew, Anakin Solo, had snuck away from the Jedi academy. They'd returned to the Great Temple in the middle of the night. Tired and dirty, Tahiri had immediately begun chattering, trying to take all the blame for the adventure, trying to keep Luke's punishment from extending to Anakin. What Luke hadn't told either of them was that they were two of the most promising students he'd ever seen. There was no way he would expel either student. They would make great Jedi Knights one day—if they could keep out of trouble long enough to learn to use the Force.

15

Trouble seemed to find Tahiri and Anakin. Only last week they'd returned bruised and battered from Yavin 8, where they'd gone to help another candidate, a Melodie named Lyric, survive her changing ceremony. While on Yavin 8, the two candidates had fought giant black rodents, vicious snakes, and a red-bristled spider that trapped its prey in thick black webs and consumed it alive. Luke Skywalker believed that experience was the best teacher in the use of the Force, but Anakin and Tahiri always rushed headlong into dangerous situations. That worried Luke. Still, their ability to use the Force to control, alter, and manipulate the energy field generated by all living things was impressive.

"I won't go," Tahiri said defiantly, stamping her bare foot down on the cool stones of the Great Temple. She'd refused to wear shoes since she'd come to Yavin 4. On her home planet Tatooine, gritty sand and a burning-hot desert were a daily reality, and foot coverings a necessity. "You won't make me go," Tahiri said again, although this time her voice faltered.

"You're right," Luke replied. He moved to the large open window in the Grand Audience Chamber. Beneath him the lush jungles of Yavin 4 steamed in the midday sun. Majestic Massassi trees, their bark a rich purplish brown, reached up toward the pyramid-shaped Great Temple. The temple was the home of future Jedi Knights, beings from across the galaxy who studied at the academy in order to one day use the Force for peace and knowledge, and in the battle against evil.

Tahiri walked over to Master Luke and stood beside his brown-robed form. She stared down at the jungle, at the greens, purples, and reds that made up a landscape she'd once dreamed about. Dreamed of in the heat and endless sand of her planet.

Luke Skywalker understood Tahiri's frustration. He, too, was originally from Tatooine. He'd spent eighteen years working on his uncle and aunt's moisture farm. The boredom had threatened to suffocate him. But there had been something else, too.

"I never knew my father," Master Luke said softly to his student. "At least not the man he was before he turned to the dark side to serve the evil emperor Palpatine. I never knew my father, Anakin Skywalker, when he was a Jedi Knight, determined to use the Force for good. And when I finally met what he'd become, Darth Vader, it was too late. It's true that he did turn from evil in his last moments, but there wasn't time for us to develop a relationship before he died." Luke paused for a moment. "Do you understand what I'm saying to you?" he asked Tahiri.

"You were an orphan in a way, too," Tahiri began slowly. "But the difference is that I won't ever have the chance to meet either of my parents. The Tusken Raiders said they're both dead."

"What about Sliven?" Luke Skywalker asked.

"He's the leader of my tribe," Tahiri answered evenly.

"Nothing more?" Luke asked.

"I guess he's the only family I'll ever have," Tahiri replied softly. "Returning to Tatooine may be the last chance I'll have to see him."

"You owe that to yourself, and to him," Master Luke said. "Still, it's your decision. I'm certain you'll make the right one." He turned and strode out of the chamber.

It's not so simple, little one, he thought as he left. Not so easy to give up the only family, the only father, you've ever known. That in itself will test all of your power, and your ability to control your own inner Force. And perhaps, just perhaps, your decision to remain at the academy will change. If that happens, we'll lose a promising student. But, as much as this would disturb me, your happiness is more important.

Luke took the turbolift down to the hangar. He found the supply ship captain, old Peckhum. Peckhum had just unloaded crates for the academy. Now he was preparing to take a delivery to a planet only hours from Tatooine. Luke asked Peckhum to prepare his ship for a detour to Tatooine the following morning. When Peckhum asked how many passengers, Luke didn't hesitate. Three, he replied. There was no way Tahiri would travel home without her best friend, Anakin Solo. And no way that Luke would allow them to go alone. Tatooine was too dangerous a planet. And Luke had a strange feeling that Tahiri's family, the Tusken Raiders, were dangerous as well.

THREE

Anakin watched Tahiri nervously finger the rough sand-colored pendant that hung from her neck. Since they'd boarded the shuttle at the academy and shot into the darkness toward the Outer Rim Territories and the planet Tatooine, Tahiri had been silent. That worried Anakin. His best friend was rarely quiet.

For a time, Anakin contented himself with thoughts of the golden globe, and the furry white Jedi Master named Ikrit that he and Tahiri had found sleeping at its base. Ikrit had discovered the globe over four hundred years ago. He'd immediately sensed that he could not break the curse, so he'd curled up beside the globe to wait for those who could. Although he knew little about the web of evil around the globe, Ikrit had a strong feeling that if an adult tried to free the golden sphere's young prisoners, the globe would shatter into a thousand shards of crystal. Anakin and Tahiri hadn't told Master Luke about the globe, its curse, or their plans to destroy the evil that had festered in the belly of the Palace of the Woolamander for thousands of years. This was something they wanted to try to handle themselves.

Tahiri was still running her small fingers over the pendant. Anakin could make out two rough prints on the surface of the oblong charm. Tahiri felt his eyes, and turned to face him.

"It was given to me by the leader of my tribe," Tahiri offered softly. She held the pendant up for Anakin to see. "There are two thumbprints in its center. Sliven told me years ago that they are my parents' prints."

"He knew your parents?" Anakin asked in surprise. Tahiri had told him she knew nothing of her family before the Tusken Raiders.

"I can only guess that he did," Tahiri replied. "But other than the pendant and those few words telling me who the thumbprints belonged to, he's never given me another clue as to who my parents were."

"But why not?" Anakin asked.

"I don't know," Tahiri answered. "I used to beg Sliven, really beg him to tell me about my mother and father. He would never answer, although I felt pain in his silence. After a few years, I stopped asking. . . ." Tahiri trailed off.

Anakin sensed his friend's torment, and her fear. "Tahiri, what are you afraid of?" he asked. "You don't have to go."

"I don't know," Tahiri said softly. "But it's more complicated than that. Sliven knew it would be, and so did Master Luke. Anakin, don't you see— I'm not like you. I don't have a brother and sister, or a mother and father who were heroes of the Rebellion. I don't know who my parents were, or how I ended up with my tribe. All I know is that the Tusken Raiders are the only family I've ever known. The only family I have. If I choose to remain at the academy, I'll lose them forever. I'll truly be an orphan." Tahiri turned to look out the shuttle window, her unseeing eyes filled with tears.

"There's more, isn't there," Anakin asked softly.

"Yes," Tahiri admitted. "I feel so mixed-up right now. I'm about to return to the only home I know. It's a place I hate and love, both at the same time. Just as I hate and love the Tusken Raiders. My life is as confusing to me as the golden globe. Except, unlike with the globe, I don't have any clue about who I really am. I don't even know if Tahiri is my real name, or just a name given to me by Sliven." Tahiri paused and gulped for air.

"Anakin, you have a family, a history. Even though being the grandson of Darth Vader frightens you, at least you know where you came from, *who* you came from. All I have are these two thumbprints. I'm afraid that if I don't return to the Raiders for good, I may never have the chance to find out who I really am. But if I do, I'm afraid I'll discover I'm meant to be something other than a Jedi Knight."

Anakin recognized the look on Tahiri's face. It was the same desperate cry for help he'd seen when, after being tossed from their silver raft, she'd thrashed in the river's water, struggling to survive. The same look she'd worn on Yavin 8 when a reel—a giant violet-colored snake—had wrapped her in its coils and tried to crush her.

The look reminded Anakin of how much they'd been through together. How much they'd learned about themselves, and their strengths in the Force. He'd used the Force to keep Tahiri from drowning in the river, and he'd actually probed within the body of the reel with his mind, to force the creature to release its hold on her. Together they'd even toppled a purella, the giant red-bristled spider with glowing orange eyes that had been poised to devour them, slowly. And then they'd learned from an elder Melodie on Yavin 8 the information that they'd needed to read the Massassi symbols in the palace and break the curse.

But to do that, they had to work together, as a team. Anakin was certain that neither of them was strong enough in the Force to wage the war alone.

"You once told me that no matter who my grandfather was, I was meant to become a Jedi Knight and use the Force for good," Anakin said softly. "The same goes for you. I understand that you want to know your history, but is it as important as the lives of the children trapped inside the golden globe? Only you can know which is more important. But whatever you decide, I'll always be your friend. . . . Okay?" Anakin said gently.

"Okay," Tahiri said with a nod.

Anakin didn't tell Tahiri that even if she chose to remain on Tatooine, he'd still attempt to break the curse. To fight the good battle, even though he knew in his heart that without Tahiri's strength he would never leave the depths of the Palace of the Woolamander alive.

"Five minutes to landing," old Peckhum transmitted back to Anakin and Tahiri. The Jedi instructor Tionne glanced back to make sure her two charges were seated. Luke Skywalker had sent her to watch over Anakin and Tahiri on Tatooine—to make sure that nothing harmed them. And that Tahiri returned to the Jedi academy, if she wished.

Anakin strapped himself in and readied himself to meet Tahiri's people. But nothing could have prepared him for what lay minutes away, beyond the safety of the shuttle's cool silver hatch.

 # FOUR

Anakin threw himself in front of Tahiri. Above him, three Tusken Raiders growled, their tall, broad forms masked in strips of white material, their faces covered with gray breath masks and dark round protective goggles. Held high in each of their hands was an axelike metal weapon with a double-edged blade that glinted beneath the harsh twin suns of Tatooine. They moved forward to attack. "Get back in the shuttle," Anakin commanded his friend. Tionne stepped forward, her silver eyes flashing. Anakin could sense the hostility and raw anger that came from the group of Raiders.

"It's all right," Tahiri said calmly. "They're from my tribe." Tahiri took a step out from behind Anakin and Tionne and moved toward the Raiders.

"Are you sure?" Anakin asked uncertainly as he

watched Tahiri walk forward. The three Raiders parted, and a fourth, who had been hidden behind them, emerged. He, too, held the axelike weapon high, and Anakin tensed. He was ready to spring forward if Tahiri needed him.

Tahiri grunted toward the fourth Raider. It was a deep, guttural sound that Anakin had never heard from his friend. The Raider growled back. "It's okay, Anakin," Tahiri said softly without turning away from the Raider. "His name is Sliven, and he's the leader of my tribe. I'm greeting him and introducing you and Tionne. Neither of you were expected—that's why the Raiders took a battle stance."

Anakin nodded, but neither he nor Tionne took their eyes off the Raiders. Sliven moved toward Tahiri, lowering his weapon as he walked. Then he let loose a string of grunts and growls, connected by a dialect Anakin could neither recognize nor understand.

"He wants to know where my robes and foot coverings are," Tahiri began.

Sliven stared down at the girl, his adoptive daughter, as she gazed up at him. Her green eyes, the color of the water he had hunted all his life, were unreadable. Then she spoke to him, making the harsh language of the Raiders sound soft.

• • •

"I just told him that one of the conditions I made when I entered the academy was that I no longer had to wear robes or shoes," Tahiri told Anakin. Her translation was cut short by several deep barks. "He says that some things never change, and my stubborn nature is one of them," Tahiri explained with a grin.

Anakin followed Tahiri and her people away from the shuttle. They'd landed at a special spot in the desert, where Tahiri had been expected. As they walked, Anakin squinted in the bright sunlight to study his surroundings. Endless yellow desert stretched out before him. Anakin had hoped they'd land in Mos Eisley, Tatooine's infamous city. Because of its remote location, Mos Eisley was known throughout the galaxy for attracting thieves, pirates, and smugglers. It was there that his father, Han Solo, first met his uncle Luke and the Jedi Master Ben Kenobi. Uncle Luke and Master Kenobi had hired his father to pilot them to Alderaan in his freighter, the *Millennium Falcon*. That was the beginning of adventures that led his father and uncle to rescue his mother, Princess Leia Organa, from the Death Star and Darth Vader, Anakin thought with pride.

The heat rolled in thick waves over the sand. Anakin felt his jumpsuit beginning to stick to his back as sweat rolled down in time to the beat of his heart. Tahiri walked in front of him, talking to

Sliven. The other three Raiders walked to the side, scanning the desert for hidden enemies. Tionne walked in silence, her large eyes never leaving the Raiders. Several times Anakin sensed danger, but the group traveled safely up and down rolling sand dunes.

Sliven's deep voice interrupted Anakin's thoughts. The Raider motioned for Anakin and Tahiri to follow him up yet another sand hill.

"Bangor!" Tahiri cried when several large, brown, furry animals came into sight. One of the animals raised his head at the sound of her voice and began to tug at the thick rope that held him to a wooden stake in the sand. Tahiri raced forward and stretched out her arms. The animal bumped his soft brown nose against her side. Tahiri reached up and scratched between his long, spiral horns. Sliven growled beside Anakin.

"He repeats that some things never change," Tahiri translated with a giggle.

Although Sliven's words sounded gruff, Anakin sensed something beneath them, a caring that he hadn't expected. After all, the Sand People, as the Tusken Raiders were also known, were famous for their aggressive, violent nature. They'd been known to attack the settlements of moisture farms on Tatooine, to steal and fight, and many times to kill. In the back of Anakin's mind, he wondered if that wasn't how Tahiri had ended up with these people. Perhaps they had attacked her

family's settlement and killed her parents.
Anakin pushed the thought away. It was too
gruesome to think that Tahiri might have lived
for most of her life with people who had killed her
parents.

"Anakin, come meet my bantha," Tahiri called
over her shoulder. Anakin walked toward the
three-meter-tall creature. "His name is Bangor,"
Tahiri began. Sliven cut in abruptly with a string
of grunts. "Sliven says that we don't name our
banthas." Tahiri turned to face the leader of her
tribe. "Well, I do," she shot back in Basic. Anakin
looked confused. "Oh, Sliven understands Basic,
although I don't know where he learned it. But he
pretends he doesn't, so I usually speak in his language," Tahiri explained slowly, so that she could
be certain Sliven understood her words. The
Raider didn't reply.

Anakin studied the bantha beside Tahiri. He'd
read that the Sand People used them as beasts of
burden, and that they could survive for weeks in
the desert without food or water. He reached up
and petted the creature. Bangor turned its large
brown eyes toward him, gently blinking long
lashes.

"Bangor is an orphan, too," Tahiri said. "He was
found wandering alone in the desert shortly after
I was found by Sliven." At that, the Raider
growled fiercely. "Sliven is angry," Tahiri explained to Anakin. "He says that I'm not an or-

phan. He says I'm a Raider, and that we've wasted enough time and must return to the tribe before dark." Tahiri frowned at Sliven, then whispered softly to Bangor. The bantha knelt, and she climbed aboard his back. Then she reached down to Anakin and pulled him up behind her. The bantha gently rose to his feet.

Sliven pulled Tionne up behind him. Then he barked, and the banthas trotted away from the outskirts of Mos Eisley toward an expanse of desert which looked endless. Anakin was suddenly overcome by the feeling that he and Tahiri were traveling into unspoken danger.

FIVE

They had been traveling for hours. Anakin felt the heat of Tatooine's twin suns beating down on his head. Tahiri had pulled the collar of her orange jumpsuit up to protect her face from blowing sand. The grit of the desert filled Anakin's mouth and eyes. There was no way to keep the sand out. Anakin wondered if this was what it was like for the young spirits trapped inside the globe. He hoped not.

An hour before, Sliven had offered the Jedi candidates some cloth to wrap their heads, and two pairs of eye protectors. Tahiri had declined for both of them, although she did accept shoes for herself. She was being difficult, but Anakin understood. His friend felt torn. Tahiri had thought it would be easy to make the decision to stay at the academy. But now that she was here, the decision would be more difficult.

No one spoke during the journey into the desert. Sliven led the group, but didn't utter a word. "Is it always this quiet?" Anakin finally whispered to Tahiri.

"Yes," she replied. "Now you can understand why I talk so much. In all my years here, I don't think I said as much as I would in one day at the academy. And don't think I didn't try," Tahiri added with a laugh. "But the only one who would ever talk to me—really talk, once I learned his language—was Sliven."

"He's not talking now," Anakin noted.

"He will," Tahiri said. "He will, because he's the reason I'm here. Sliven is the leader of our tribe, but he's more than that. He's the one who found me. The Sand People are nomads, traveling in small tribes within the harsh desert. They're experts at survival, because above all else they're practical. The weak are left to die. Only the strong, those who can care for themselves, are part of the tribe. And outsiders, any outsiders, are of no concern. Especially children who don't belong to the tribe."

"But you were an outsider, an orphan child," Anakin interrupted.

"Yes," Tahiri said softly. "And for some reason Sliven chose to take me into his tribe. To care for me in the only way he knew how. I didn't grow up with a father or mother like you did, Anakin. But Sliven was as close to a father as I'll ever know.

He taught me how to scavenge for food and water, how to train and ride a bantha. And how to fight with a gaderffii stick.

"Sliven knows that if I choose to remain at the academy the tribe will refuse to take me back. I think that having me return to make my decision was Sliven's way of giving me one last chance to remain with the tribe, and with him."

"It sounds like he truly cares for you," Anakin offered.

"Cares?" Tahiri weighed the word thoughtfully. "In his own way, I know he does. But he's never cared enough to give me the one thing in my life that I wanted. He has never told me the story of how he found me. And if he truly cared, he would give me my history," Tahiri ended sadly.

"Are you sure he knows?" Anakin asked.

"I've sensed all my life that he knows more than he's said," Tahiri replied.

Sliven barked once, and the banthas halted at the top of a large sand dune. Anakin looked around them. There was nothing in sight—no structures, no other Raiders.

"Can you feel them?" Tahiri whispered to her friend.

"Who?" Anakin whispered back.

"The tribe—they're all here," she replied. And, as if on cue, some twenty Raiders topped the sand dune to the left of the group. Silently they walked toward the Jedi candidates. Tahiri commanded

Bangor down, and the bantha knelt so that she and Anakin could drop to the ground. Tahiri stood erect, her blonde hair blown back from her face by the licks of a hot evening breeze. The suns were beginning to set, casting a pale pink shadow along the dunes.

Anakin watched his friend as she faced her tribe. There was confusion in her large green eyes, but there was also a resolve he hadn't seen there before. The Raiders who had traveled with them moved to join the rest of their tribe. All except Sliven. He stood one meter to the right of Tahiri.

A female Raider's voice rose from the group and spoke. "Her name is Vexa," Tahiri said, not trying to hide her dislike. "She says welcome home." The Raider stepped forward. She, too, was covered from head to toe; only her voice indicated that she was a woman. "She says that they did not expect me to return. They did not expect me to fulfill the promise."

"What promise?" Anakin asked under his breath. He sensed that Tahiri was uncertain, but his friend said nothing.

The Raider continued in her strange, rough dialect. Tionne stepped forward. Seeing Anakin's confusion, she began to translate. "Sliven said you would come, that you would fulfill the promise he made many years ago. I myself am sorry to see you, for two reasons. First, I do not think you will survive, and the tribe will gain nothing by your death. Second, if you do survive, Sliven will remain the leader of our tribe.

"There are many of us who do not wish to follow Sliven. Years ago he showed his weakness. He brought an outsider into our tribe, one who was a child and could not add to our strength. If you survive, you will prove that Sliven was right, that you did grow into an adult member of our tribe. If that is the case, Sliven will continue to lead us. If not, he will die, for that is the promise he made." Tionne paused.

"You knew this," Tahiri said in a flat voice as she turned toward Sliven. "You made this promise and never told me about it. All my life you taught me how to survive in the desert, and I thought you taught me as your own, as one you cared for, maybe even loved. But you taught me so that one day I could fulfill a promise you made without my permission—a promise that might end my life or save your own." Sliven was silent.

"What did he promise?" Tahiri quietly asked Vexa. As Vexa spoke, Tionne translated for Anakin.

"You will be taken deep into the Dune Sea, which borders the Jundland Wastes. It is the place you were found, a desolate place not often visited by Sand People. You will be left there without food or water, alone—or if you prefer, with the boy. I suggest you go alone—there is some chance that your skills may enable you to survive, but the boy is not from Tatooine, and he will be a burden to you. You will be left to find your way back to this tribe. To do so will mean using your strength and wits to find your way safely through the Dune Sea, across the mountains and the canyons of the Jundland Wastes, and then through the harsh, hot desert.

"You have one week. During that time we will remain in this exact spot. If you do not return to the tribe in that time, we will know that you have either been captured by enemies or have not survived. Whatever, if you return to the tribe later than seven days from your departure, you will also have failed to fulfill the terms of the promise. But Tahiri—you do not have to do this." Tahiri thought for a moment, then spoke.

"What happens if I don't?" she asked.

Tionne gave Tahiri an incredulous look. How could the child even consider agreeing to such a thing? If Luke Skywalker had known that this was why Sliven had asked that she be returned, he would never have allowed Tahiri to go back to Tatooine, Tionne thought. And there was no way she would allow the child to fulfill Sliven's promise. Tahiri's safety was Tionne's responsibility.

"What happens?" Tahiri asked again. This time Sliven slowly answered in Basic.

"You will be returned to your ship," Sliven said. "And then shuttled back to the Jedi academy."

"And you'll be put to death," Tahiri said more to the tribe than to Sliven. Sliven nodded. "Why should I attempt to fulfill the promise?" Tahiri asked Sliven as she turned to face him. Her green eyes glowered from beneath ash blonde brows.

Sliven replied slowly. There was sadness in his voice. "Years ago I did what I did to save your life. You may not believe that right now, but there was no other way for me to persuade the tribe to accept you."

"Even given that," Tahiri said quietly to Sliven, "why should I risk my life now so that you can live?"

"Because even if you do die," Sliven replied, "you will do so with the knowledge you've sought all your life: the history of your family, of who you really are." Sliven moved forward, placed both hands on Tahiri's shoulders, and looked into her eyes with his own darkly goggled ones. "That, too, was part of the deal, little one. You could only be told your history if you accepted the promise."

"Why?" Anakin interrupted. "That's cruel!"

"I agree, Anakin, the bargain was cruel," Sliven said. "But telling Tahiri her history was to be a reward of sorts from the tribe if she ever chose to fulfill the promise. And not telling Tahiri until that point was a punishment to me from the tribe. They knew she would ask, and that I would want to tell her the truth. They knew it would be difficult for me to keep Tahiri's history from her—that it would take the strength they had begun to believe I lacked."

"Tell me my history," Tahiri said with glowing eyes. "I accept the promise."

"No!" Anakin cried out. But he couldn't stop the words from leaving Tahiri's mouth, any more than he could take them back once they had settled heavily on the sand.

SIX

Anakin glowered at Tahiri. How could she agree to the deal Sliven had struck? How could she put her life in danger, and the lives of thousands inside the globe? Then he remembered what he'd told her on the shuttle only hours before. He'd said that no matter what happened on Tatooine, he would support her. Tahiri might beat the odds Vexa had spoken of and survive. If that happened, she'd finally know her history. And, perhaps that would give her the peace of mind she needed to forever leave the Raiders and return to the academy. Anakin stared off across the endless sea of sand. "I'm going with you," he finally said to Tahiri.

"She might be right," Tahiri replied with a nod at Vexa. "I do know about survival in the desert—although I've never had to live without the tribe.

You don't know anything. It's going to be hard enough for me without you tagging along."

"Stop, Tahiri," Anakin interrupted. "It doesn't matter what I know about the desert. I'm good with the Force and a great problem solver. We're a team, and that's the end of the discussion." Tahiri nodded, then turned to Sliven.

"Wait," Tionne said in disbelief. "If you think I'm going to allow either of you to accept this deal, you're very wrong. Neither of you are going into the desert, and that's final," she said sternly.

"Tahiri's made her decision," Sliven interrupted. "Tionne, the tribe will not allow you to interfere. You will remain with us for one week. If the children don't return, we will take you back to the spot you've agreed to meet your shuttle pilot."

Tionne's silver eyes clouded with worry. There were too many Raiders to fight. "Tahiri, please rethink your decision," she said with forced calm.

"Tell me my history," Tahiri said to Sliven. Her voice was a command. Sliven nodded, then led Anakin and Tahiri away from the tribe. Tionne watched the three walk away. There was absolutely nothing she could do to stop them.

Vexa called out from behind them. "She says we leave at dawn," Tahiri murmured. Anakin turned toward the female Raider. Although he couldn't see her face, he was sure that she was smirking. And he could sense that she was pleased by

Tahiri's choice. There was an old hatred inside of her that Anakin could almost taste.

When they had moved from the tribe, Sliven gestured for Tahiri and Anakin to sit. They settled across from the Raider in the cooling sands of the desert. Sliven pushed several tattered blankets toward the Jedi candidates. Now that the sun had set, a chilly breeze blew across the desert. Soon the frigid night that Tatooine was known for would wrap them in its cold hands. Anakin and Tahiri covered themselves with the blankets. Then, in a voice full of years, sand, and sorrow, the Raider began Tahiri's story.

"Your father's name was Tryst Veila, your mother's was Cassa. They were moisture farmers on Tatooine," Sliven began. "As you know, we have always lived in uneasy peace with the farmers on this planet. Your parents were no different. No different, except that for a small moment in time I knew them—and cared for them.

"Almost six years ago to this day, there was a battle between my tribe and a group of smugglers who were hiding from their enemies in the desert. These smugglers tried to steal our food and water, and I was hurt in the battle. When the fight ended, I had been separated from my tribe and wounded to the point of near death. I had lost my bantha and was traveling by foot in the desert when I saw your parents' farm. I had lost blood, and hadn't had water in several days. I crawled to their doorway. Your mother, Cassa, found me passed out several meters from her front door. She dragged me inside her home, peeled away my robes, and treated my wounds.

"It took almost two months for me to heal. Several times in the first weeks I almost died, and I would have if not for Cassa and Tryst. They showed me kindness I never knew existed.

"Tahiri, you were not quite three years old when your parents cared for me. I remember your mother running her fingers through your blonde hair, the same color as hers. And I can see your father, his laughing green eyes the shape of your own. And you—you were fascinated by my eye protectors and the cloth of my robes. You would crawl onto my sleeping pad and giggle as you traced my goggles or wound my tattered robe around your fingers. And it was from both you and your parents that I learned to understand and speak Basic. That is what later helped me to teach you the language of the Raiders.

"It took two months for me to heal. During that time Tryst and Cassa cared for me. They fed me and tended my wounds, and allowed me to play with their daughter—a being full of light and happiness. When I was strong enough, I helped your mother with light chores. One day, I even fashioned Tryst his own gaderffii and taught him how to fight with it. He learned quickly—it was strange how he fought, sensing my movements almost before I made them, just as Cassa could feel my emotions without hearing me speak."

"They were both sensitive to the Force," Anakin said quietly.

Sliven nodded. "Since that time with Tryst and Cassa, I have often thought the same thing," he said. "For I saw the identical abilities in Tahiri that I noticed in her parents. That is why I wasn't surprised when the Jedi Master, Luke Skywalker, and the Jedi Knight, Tionne, asked to take Tahiri to their academy. I knew that the Force was in her blood—and I let her go with the Jedi because I couldn't deny her that tie with her parents."

Sliven turned back to Tahiri and paused before he began again. Anakin could sense that the Raider was in pain. Tahiri leaned forward, caught by his words.

"As I said, I taught your father how to fight with the gaderffii. Soon he could beat me without even trying. And it wasn't because I was still wounded—in those months with your parents I had regained most of my strength. My hesitation to leave is one of the reasons that Cassa and Tryst were killed. You see, I didn't know that my tribe was still searching for me. But one of the wounded had seen me trudge away from the battle. And it is my people's way to search for a wounded leader before they name another.

"The morning my tribe found me, Tryst and I

were sparring with our gaderffii. He was winning, of course—I can still hear your mother's laughter as she watched us. It was a moment of happiness, being there with them. And then the air was filled with battle cries. Moments later your parents were dead. My tribe had thought that I was being attacked, and they had struck to save my life.

"I remember standing there and hearing your shrill cry from inside the farmhouse. It was almost as if you knew, as if you felt your parents' death. I raced inside and picked you up. Vexa followed me. 'Leave her to die,' she instructed. 'You are back with your tribe now.' And that is why I made the bargain. I didn't make it out of selfishness. It was the only way I knew to save you. And the years I spent training you to live with the tribe were not spent so that you could one day keep the promise and save my life. I taught you as a father. . . ." Sliven's voice finally broke.

"Finish," Anakin said softly to Sliven. The Raider began to speak again.

"I made the bargain with my tribe that afternoon as we sat outside your farmhouse. We argued fiercely. 'Leave her,' they said. 'She is not one of us.' Vexa was driven half crazy by my idea of bringing you into the tribe. She said that I was weak, not fit to be a leader. But I couldn't leave you, not after your parents' kindness and my fondness for you. So I agreed to the terms of a promise Vexa thought up. You would live with us, during which time I would be responsible for you. When you were nine years old, the age when Raider children are considered full working members of the tribe, you would have to leave us or fulfill the promise to show you belonged.

"If you refused, we planned to take you to Mos Eisley and leave you in the city. There, you'd have to find work, a family, or a friend to care for you. The chances of that would have been slim. I was secretly relieved when you were invited to the Jedi academy. That meant that you would have another choice if you decided that the deal I struck was too difficult to accept. If you chose to honor the promise, I would be allowed to tell you your history. If you did not survive, or refused the bargain, I would give up my life.

"Before we left the farmhouse, I made a thick paste and pressed Cassa's and Tryst's thumbs into it to make a print. When the paste set, I carved it into a pendant and placed it on a strip of leather. It was the only way I could give you something of your parents.

"I knew that this moment would come. That you would learn that I was the cause of your parents' death, and that I made a promise to save your life, which bought you six more years, but years of not knowing your own history. Still, I don't think I could ever have prepared myself for the hatred you must feel for me. Perhaps I am as weak as Vexa believes me to be, after all."

Tahiri studied the Raider who had been a father to her, the only father she remembered. She thought of her parents, whom she'd just learned had been very much in love, and who had died because of a misunderstanding. Her fingers caressed the thumbprints of her pendant, and then she spoke.

"I don't hate you, Sliven," Tahiri began. "You didn't strike my parents down. And those who did thought they were protecting you. My parents cared for you because they chose to, just as you chose to care for me. And I know now that you cared," Tahiri added. "One other thing: Caring doesn't make you weak—it's what made my parents' love strong, and what makes my friendship with Anakin strong." Tahiri paused to understand the jumble of her thoughts before she continued.

"What I choose to do now isn't on your shoulders, Sliven," Tahiri stated. "You bought me my life, and now what I do with that life is my decision. I've accepted, not because I had to, but because I know it's the right thing for me to do. I owe you thanks for my life, and for being the man I know as my father. And if I survive, I want your thumbprint in a pendant next to those of my parents."

Anakin met his friend's gaze. He was surprised by her ability to understand Sliven's motives. There was no anger in her voice, only acceptance and peace. Sliven rose and nodded at Tahiri before he left the two Jedi candidates alone. It was clear that Tahiri had deeply moved him.

Anakin reached over and touched Tahiri's shoulder as he watched crystal tears run slowly down her face. They were sad tears, but at the same time they were good. Tahiri now knew who she was, and in the knowing she was free to become a Jedi Knight, if she chose.

SEVEN

Massive hands gripped the front of Anakin's Jedi academy jumpsuit and hauled him to his feet. He shook his grogginess off like a bad dream and prepared to fight. Tahiri, too, was ripped to a standing position. Anakin's ice blue eyes swept over the situation. They were surrounded by Raiders, who growled and snarled madly. "Tahiri," he said roughly, "are you all right?"

"Fine," Tahiri replied in a voice still coated with sleep.

Together they were pushed toward Sliven, who sat alone in the sands. What is going on? Anakin thought, trying to control the confusion he felt at their treatment.

"It must be time," Tahiri replied.

Anakin saw that pale pink scribbles of dawn had bathed the golden sands in soft rose. Some wake-up call, he thought grumpily. Sliven nodded once at Anakin and Tahiri, then allowed five Raiders to take them to their waiting banthas. The large animals stood silently, their long, shaggy brown coats curling down to the sand. The Jedi candidates were barely settled aboard Bangor when a loud grunt signaled the banthas to ride. Anakin noted that Tahiri didn't look back at Sliven as they started across the dunes with a dull kick of sand. He didn't see Tionne watching as they raced off, a small humanoid Jedi Knight surrounded by a crowd of Raiders. If Anakin had seen Tionne, he would have been alarmed at the look of worry and fear written across her features.

A day passed, then another. The only sounds in the desert were the crunch of bantha hooves. The terrain stretched out endlessly as Bangor followed the five Raiders deeper into the desert. The group stopped twice each day—once during the sweltering heat of midday to sip water and eat brown lumps of food, which tasted vile and which Anakin didn't want identified, and at night, when the suns set and the desert became so cold that his fingers grew numb. Then Anakin huddled with Tahiri beneath the thin blanket the Raiders provided.

That afternoon, the group had climbed quickly through low, sand-colored mountains. Anakin had sensed fear in the fierce Raiders. He'd been too hot and tired to ask Tahiri what they could

possibly be afraid of. Now, as they lay against
Bangor for warmth beneath the dark covers of the
night sky, Anakin was once again too exhausted
to talk. He watched Tahiri scratch her bantha's
scruffy neck. The creature stared at Tahiri with
soft brown eyes, and Anakin could sense the bond
between them. He fell off into a dreamless sleep.
Thoughts of how he and Tahiri were going to survive in the desert without food and water slid un-
answered to the sand. They would wait in this
spot until tomorrow.

There was no water in the Dune Sea. Not that
Anakin had expected any as they traveled
through the sea—a vast desert expanse that
stretched thousands of kilometers. It was hard to
believe that an area could be more barren than
the desert and the Jundland Wastes. But the
Dune Sea was, Anakin thought bleakly as he
scanned the never-ending sand. Midway through
the third day, the Raiders began to travel more
slowly, cautiously. What could be dangerous out
here? Anakin wondered. His thoughts were cut
short when one of the Raiders barked and all the
banthas halted. Must be time for lunch, he
thought without relish.

Anakin slid off Bangor and gave Tahiri a hand
down. The heat of the day hadn't lessened with
the onset of afternoon. Tahiri's hair was matted
down with sweat, and her lips had begun to crack
from the beating rays of the suns. As the two chil-

dren sank to the ground, one of the Raiders grabbed Bangor's lead rope and drew the bantha toward him. Then, in a flash, the Raiders re- mounted their banthas and tore away from Anakin and Tahiri, bathing them in a prickling shower of sand. Neither moved as they watched the Raiders race into the distance. They saw Ban- gor struggle to pull away from the line, to return to Tahiri, but he was held firmly to the group. The Raiders topped a dune and disappeared from view.

Anakin scanned the Dune Sea through squint- ing eyes. He and Tahiri sat in the center of an unending desert. Above them the twin suns of Tatooine beat down relentlessly. There were no life-forms in sight. Just sun and sand. Sand and sun. "Any suggestions?" Anakin asked Tahiri.

"By night, the tracks left by the banthas will be covered by blowing sand," Tahiri began. "Let's fol- low them until they disappear. At least that'll head us in the right direction."

"It's a start," Anakin said feebly. "What about food and water?"

Tahiri replied, "That will depend on what we come across." There was a hard glint in her green eyes.

Anakin couldn't help remembering something he'd read about the Sand People. Survival was the rule. Survival at all costs. He began to trudge beside Tahiri. They rose and fell over the dunes, their eyes never leaving the bantha prints, which were already beginning to fade beneath the blowing sands. Hours passed, and the twin suns of Tatooine began to set. And then, without warning, the trail disappeared and Anakin and Tahiri were left alone, truly alone.

Or were they? Anakin wondered as a sense of danger raced down his spine like lightning. Were they alone?

EIGHT

The sand beneath Anakin's feet began to shift. Before he had the chance to run, the desert floor rumbled and shook. Tahiri lost her balance and fell beside him, then began to roll downward, toward a pit of sand several meters away that neither Jedi candidate had noticed in the fading light. "What's happening?" Anakin yelled.

Tahiri's hands clawed at the sand as she continued to slide away from her friend. Her small fingers ran through the grains like water. Then her legs dropped over the edge of the pit, and in a flash she disappeared from view.

Anakin threw himself forward, staring into the pit. Tahiri's fall had been broken by a small dirt ledge, a meter from the edge. Anakin reached for her, his fingers just managing to grasp her hand. He tried to pull her back up the sandy hill, but it was all he could do to hold her in place. Tahiri's frightened green eyes locked on Anakin's. He pulled harder, and slowly he began to draw her out of the pit. Tahiri dug her knees into the dirt walls and scrambled up the sliding terrain.

Suddenly, Tahiri's feet shot out from beneath her. She struggled as she lost her footing, then gave a small cry as she slid back down to the ledge.

"Give me your hand!" Anakin called to his friend. Tahiri reached up again. But something made her turn the instant before their fingers met. When she did, fear rolled over her in a tidal wave and she dropped to her knees and out of Anakin's reach.

A thick, puce-colored tentacle emerged from the depths of the pit and snaked through the air. Tahiri froze in terror. The tentacle whipped through the pit, searching for the prey it had sensed. Three more tentacles snaked upward and joined the first. "Tahiri, grab my hand!" Anakin cried. Still his friend didn't move. I can't reach her, Anakin thought with growing frustration and terror.

Anakin crawled forward on his stomach, dug his toes into the sand, and leaned into the pit. He reached down and grabbed at Tahiri's jumpsuit. The creature in the pit sensed his movement, and tentacles lashed toward the Jedi candidates. Anakin stopped breathing, his fingers frozen on

Tahiri's suit. The tentacles brushed along the walls of the pit, searching, searching.

I've got to get her out of here, Anakin thought. He could barely control his panic as he watched the tentacles draw nearer. Tahiri slowly turned to her friend. "What is it?" Anakin mouthed to Tahiri.

Tahiri shook her head. She had no idea what the creature was, only that it wanted to wrap them in its tentacles and draw them downward.

It doesn't matter what it is, Anakin thought. He could sense the creature's hunger.

"Climb," Anakin mouthed to Tahiri. She didn't move. She was frozen in panic, her green eyes were fixed on the tentacles as they danced through the air.

Anakin tightened his grip on Tahiri's arms until she turned to face him again. "Climb," he said again. This time his ice blue eyes flashed, and his word was a command that rang with the power of the Force. Immediately, Tahiri turned and began to scramble up the dirt and sand wall behind her. Anakin drew her up, helping her keep her balance when she slid. He could sense the creature's tentacles moving toward them. The moment Tahiri's hands reached the edge of the pit, Anakin leaned back and yanked her out. Then they ran.

Anakin and Tahiri ran until the creature and the pit were four dunes behind them and their lungs ached. And when they fell to the sand, gasping for breath and sweating in the stillness of the desert night, they didn't notice the cold. All they saw was the beauty of the stars, and all they felt was the relief of their own freedom. And when sleep swept over them like the blowing of the desert sand, they gave themselves up to its hands.

NINE

Anakin awoke, facedown, in the warm desert sands of Tatooine. He felt his belly rumbling in hunger, and his throat burned with thirst. Sand clung to his eyelashes and crusted along his mouth. He reached up to wipe the grains from his face. His senses came alive. He smelled their company before he saw them.

"Anakin, we've got a slight problem," Tahiri said softly as she rolled to face her friend. She motioned with her head toward the brown-robed creatures that stood in a circle around them.

"What are they?" Anakin asked as he wrinkled his nose. Whatever the beings were, they smelled rotten, he thought.

"Jawas," Tahiri whispered.

Anakin remembered hearing about the scavenger race from his uncle Luke. Jawas were rodent-like beings that traveled in bands, searching for wrecked ships to salvage, vehicles to steal, and discarded hardware to collect. Anakin studied the meter-tall creatures. There were ten of them, and they jabbered and pointed at him and Tahiri, their yellow eyes glowing.

"I think they're trying to figure out if we're worth something or if they should just leave us in the desert," Anakin said. If the Jawas left them, he thought, he and Tahiri would die of thirst, hunger, and exposure. The Jawas moved toward the two Jedi. Tahiri rose to her feet.

"Careful," Anakin whispered.

"They aren't really dangerous," Tahiri said softly. "In fact, they usually like humans, because we're the ones they sell their scavenged material to."

"I'd be willing to bet that we don't exactly look like paying customers," Anakin grumbled as he stood up.

The Jawas quickly decided that Anakin and Tahiri weren't worth bothering with and began to walk away. "Strange that they're walking," Tahiri murmured. "They usually travel in sandcrawlers."

"What are sandcrawlers?" Anakin asked with interest.

"They're huge ore haulers that human miners brought to Tatooine years ago. They expected to make a fortune in the Wastelands. But they discovered that there's not much worth mining out here. So, they left the haulers and the Jawas took them. Jawas use the sandcrawlers to find and collect metals and wrecked machinery. The deserts here are full of junk. Galactic battles have been fought near Tatooine for hundreds of years. And whatever falls from space and lands here is preserved by the dry climate. Jawas find wrecked ships, droids, and other machinery, which they fix and sell in Mos Eisley or to moisture farmers in the desert." Tahiri watched silently as the Jawas walked away from them. "Anakin, let's follow them," she suggested with a glint in her eye. "Wherever they're camped, there's got to be food and water."

Anakin and Tahiri began to tag along with the Jawas. If they noticed, they didn't turn around. "At least we're heading toward the Jundland Wastes," Anakin noted with a nod toward the mountain peaks that had appeared as they crested a dune.

"So why do they smell so bad?" Anakin asked Tahiri as they trudged through the sand.

"Sliven once told me that the Jawas love their smell," Tahiri began. "They use scent to identify each other, to sense health, anger, or sadness. To us, they stink. But to them, scent is information."

"I wonder what information they got about us," Anakin said. He didn't need Tahiri to answer. Fear, hunger, thirst, confusion; that about summed up their smells.

Over an hour later, the Jawas stopped walking. "Must be home sweet home," Anakin said as he spied what had to be a sandcrawler. The machine was a dull brown, its hull ravaged by wind storms and the suns' rays. "If they've got that thing, why walk for hours in the sand?" Anakin asked Tahiri.

"It must not be working," Tahiri said as she squinted at the sandcrawler. "Sandcrawlers are pretty old. And even though Jawas are good mechanics, sometimes a machine just stops working and can't be fixed."

"I bet I could fix it," Anakin said softly as he walked toward the vehicle. The Jawas let out alarmed cries and raced to block Anakin's path to the sandcrawler. "That is," Anakin added, "if they'd let me near it."

"Hey, guys," Anakin said with a smile. "I'm not going to hurt your sandcrawler, I just want to try to fix it for you." He watched as one of the Jawas lifted a canteen to his lips and drank deeply before passing the water to another. "How about if I fix it, and you guys give my friend and me some of that water?" Anakin wheedled. The Jawas didn't reply. In fact, they ignored him.

Anakin thought about the time Tahiri had been drowning in the river on Yavin 4 and he'd used his voice and the Force to command her to struggle, to swim. Could he do the same thing with the Jawas?

Tahiri saw the glint in Anakin's ice blue eyes. "What is it?" she asked.

"I was just thinking that maybe I could use the Force to command the Jawas to let me into their sandcrawler. If I can fix it, maybe they'll give us a ride to the Jundland Wastes, and some food and water . . . It's a dumb idea, right?" Anakin said in embarrassment.

Tahiri replied slowly. "You've done it before, and I think it's our best chance. You've got to try." Tahiri gave a sharp whistle and the Jawas turned to face the Jedi students.

"Here goes nothing," Anakin murmured as he faced the Jawas. "Let me into the sandcrawler," he said in a soft voice.

The Jawas jabbered, but still blocked Anakin's path. It was clear that the sandcrawler, working or not, was their most valued possession.

"Let me pass," Anakin said more strongly. One of the Jawas moved aside, but the others let out a string of sounds and the creature stopped in his tracks. It's not working, Anakin said to himself in frustration. His throat burned from speaking, and his head felt light with hunger. I've got to calm myself, got to believe that I can succeed, he thought. Anakin closed his eyes, and the next time he spoke his voice carried the power of the Force. "LET ME PASS, NOW!" he called. The Jawas moved aside.

Anakin walked toward the vehicle, his ice blue

eyes glinting in the midday sun. He climbed inside and disappeared from view. Tahiri trotted after her friend and followed him inside the sandcrawler.

It reeked. Anakin tried not to gag at the stink inside the vehicle. He sensed that Tahiri, too, was trying not to let the smell overcome her. Anakin had never been inside a sandcrawler, but he'd also never seen anything mechanical that he couldn't figure out. When he was only two, he'd amazed his brother and sister, the twins Jaina and Jacen, by taking apart a droid and putting it back together. He quickly found the control panel deep within the vehicle and began to tinker.

"Can you fix it?" Tahiri asked her friend.

Anakin ran his hands along the tangle of cables and wires that trailed from the control panel. "I think I've found the problem," he began excitedly. "There's a short circuit in a connector." Anakin studied one of the cables. Its surface was slightly darker than the rest. "It's this one," he murmured.

"Tahiri, can you find me another cable in that junk?" Anakin asked with a wave of his hand toward the pile of broken-down droids and machinery the Jawas had collected.

Tahiri began to rummage through the metal scraps. "Will this work?" she asked as she held up a meter-long cable.

"No," Anakin replied. "Its got to be longer."

Several minutes later Tahiri held up two more cables. Anakin selected one and replaced the burned out cable. "Let's see if this will do the trick," Anakin said softly. He connected the cable to the control panel, then leaned over to push the sandcrawler's start-up button. With a deep, rasping rumble the sandcrawler hummed to life. Anakin and Tahiri emerged, to the cheers of the Jawas.

The Jedi candidates were handed water jugs and brown lumps of food. They drank deeply, the liquid soothing their throats and splashing into empty bellies. When they'd eaten their fill, Tahiri turned to the Jawas and thanked them. Then she pointed at the Jundland Wastes, at herself and Anakin, and at the sandcrawler. The Jawas understood, and beckoned Anakin and Tahiri toward the sandcrawler. Soon the Jawas and the Jedi candidates were headed for the craggy mountains in the distance. And the smell that had tightened their stomachs no longer made Anakin and Tahiri feel sick. Now it was the smell of new friends.

Anakin stared out the window plate of the sandcrawler. The Jundland Wastes loomed before him, its jagged rocks and canyons signaling that too soon the ride would be over and they would once again be traveling by foot. Beyond those canyons, Anakin thought, is Tahiri's tribe. And we have five more days to find them. His thoughts wandered as the twin suns of Tatooine set over the desert, transforming its glittering golden sands into darkness.

TEN

The sandcrawler reached the scattered rocks that signaled the beginning of the Jundland Wastes on their third morning in the desert. The Jawas drove the battered sandcrawler until they could no longer navigate the rocks, then ground to a halt.

"Thank you," Anakin said to the Jawas as he and Tahiri prepared to leave the sandcrawler. One of the Jawas grabbed his arm. "What is it, little guy?" Anakin asked. "Don't you want us to leave?" Anakin sensed that the Jawa wanted to tell him something. Maybe he smelled Anakin's and Tahiri's confusion and fear. Maybe he smelled danger in the distance. Unfortunately, Anakin couldn't understand the Jawa's speech. And neither could Tahiri.

Finally, the Jawa filled two rough cloth packs with food and water and handed them to the Jedi candidates. Once again, Anakin and Tahiri thanked their new friends. Then they climbed out of the sandcrawler and into the beginning of the Jundland Wastes. One of the Jawas called out after them, and they caught two gaderffii sticks that were tossed through the air. The Jawas must have recognized the smell of bantha and Raiders on Anakin's and Tahiri's clothes and skin.

Tahiri and Anakin hoisted the makeshift packs onto their backs. They used the gaderffii sticks to help them walk along the rocks. And, although he didn't ask, Anakin sensed that these were weapons they might need.

"Tahiri, I need to stop for a minute," Anakin gasped several hours later. The travel was strenuous, and it was taking its toll. Tahiri was used to the heat, the sun, the dry climate. For Anakin, who'd lived his whole life in the city of Coruscant, Tatooine was a harsh planet. Tahiri handed Anakin a jug of water, and he drank sparingly. Both Jedi candidates ate some of the brownish lumps of food. Then they began traveling again, bathed in the glare of the sun.

A high-pitched scream filled the air. "Tahiri," Anakin whispered behind his friend, amazed that she hadn't stopped at the horrific cry. "What was that?"

"That was the scream of a womp rat," Tahiri said quietly. "But it wasn't about to attack us. That was the cry of a wounded rat. I know the sound—I've fought a lot of rodents over the years."

Anakin and Tahiri wound their way along the canyons of the Jundland Wastes, the desert beyond now in sight and within their grasp. But Anakin sensed a growing fear in Tahiri. And he again had the disturbing feeling that they were not alone.

Several high-pitched screams filled the air, so bloodcurdling and drawn-out that Anakin and Tahiri both dropped to the ground behind a large rock. "More womp rats," Tahiri whispered. This time the screams had shaken her.

Anakin started to rise. He'd fight the rodents with his gaderffii stick if they were going to attack.

"Those were death cries," Tahiri said, sensing Anakin's intentions. "Something killed them."

"Another rat?" Anakin asked hopefully.

"I don't think so," Tahiri replied. "They rarely attack each other."

"Let's get out of here," Anakin said, grabbing Tahiri's arm and pulling her up. "Whatever's out there, we don't want to wait for it to find us."

"It's a krayt dragon," Tahiri said, her voice dripping with dread. "I've sensed something following us for the last hour."

Krayt dragons were large carnivorous reptiles that lived in the mountains surrounding Tatooine's Jundland Wastes. Some thought that the dragons no longer existed, that they'd become extinct when settlers came to Tatooine, exposing them to various infections as well as hunting them for food and trophies.

"I thought krayt dragons were pretty rare," Anakin said to Tahiri.

"Tell that to the one stalking us right now," Tahiri replied with fear.

ELEVEN

All thoughts were wiped out of Anakin's mind
as a rock-crushing roar filled the air. And this
time, it was not the sound of a womp rat. This
time it was full of the venom of a different creature. A creature that towered over the Jedi candidates, its massive jaws spread open to reveal a
red forked tongue and rows of black teeth that
glistened with the greenish ooze of womp rat
blood.

"Krayt dragon," Anakin said grimly. The beast
was perched on the rocks above them, its head
covered with seven black horns, its back ridged
with sharp bony nodules and a jagged dorsal
spine. The creature's scaly green body was tipped
with claws of crimson that matched its reddish
eyes—angry eyes, divided by black slit-shaped
pupils that stared intently from Anakin to Tahiri
and back again.

Anakin slowly stood. "Leave us alone," he commanded in a voice touched with fear and only weakly ringing with the Force. The krayt dragon hissed, but made no move to leave the Jedi candidates. "LEAVE US!" Anakin called out. The dragon screeched, then struck out like lightning, one massive limb batting Anakin into the air. He landed on the rocks, ten meters from where he'd stood. The dragon's claws had ripped through his academy jumpsuit and made five bloody gashes across his rib cage. The sliced skin burned, but Anakin sensed that his wounds weren't deep. "I'm all right, Tahiri," he called. That's when he heard her scream.

Anakin bolted to his feet in time to see the monster moving in on Tahiri. "Stop!" he cried. But the reptile kept advancing toward his friend. "Fight him, Tahiri!" Anakin yelled.

Tahiri rose and tried to strike the dragon with her gaderffii. The creature's crimson eyes flashed as it batted the weapon from Tahiri's grip. Then Tahiri was covered by the dragon's dark shadow. Anakin scrambled across the rocks. He had to save his friend. The dragon turned as he approached. Tahiri was pinned beneath its front legs. The monster's red tongue flicked toward Anakin, as if tasting him. "Let her go!" Anakin growled at the loathsome creature.

The dragon charged Anakin, its eyes flashing. Anakin's ice blue eyes narrowed as he stared at the advancing monster. There has got to be a way to defeat it, he thought. But a split second later the creature grasped him in its jaw and turned to romp rapidly through the canyon.

Tahiri bolted to her feet. To save Anakin, she had to trail the krayt dragon. She ripped her pack off her back and tore after the beast. It would take all her strength to keep up with the creature, but if she lost sight of it, she wouldn't be able to help her friend.

So, you've decided Anakin is enough for dinner, Tahiri thought grimly as she climbed after the creature. She could feel Anakin's fear as he was carried away. Tahiri raced through the rocks. She only hoped the dragon's lair wasn't far away; the pace was quickly wearing her down. I won't let you down, Anakin, Tahiri thought. There are all kinds of strength—that's what Master Ikrit once told me. And I'm going to find the one that will defeat the dragon.

If the creature sensed her as she followed, it didn't let on. In fact, it seemed to have completely forgotten Tahiri existed. She wondered if the krayt lost its desire to hunt and kill once it found its prey. Tahiri followed the dragon for fifteen minutes as it wound along the rocky canyon. Her breath escaped in ragged streams. She was exhausted, but she wouldn't stop to rest until she had saved Anakin. The monster was widening the distance between them, and Tahiri forced herself to quicken her pace. She hoped that wherever it was heading, there wouldn't be any more dragons. Fighting one was going to be hard enough.

Suddenly, the dragon disappeared. Tahiri's heart sank. Had she fallen so far behind that she'd lost the creature? She stared in every direction—there was no sign of the dragon or Anakin. Her shoulders sagged in defeat and she slowly sat down on a large boulder. Her eyes filled with tears and she angrily shook her head to get rid of the unwanted saltwater.

Out of the corner of one eye, Tahiri noticed a dark hole between two large rocks. She leapt forward. From out of the hole rose an oily smell that burned her eyes and made her gag. She crouched and peered down. She couldn't see anything in the blackness. Tahiri grabbed the rough edges of the hole and dropped in, her body sliding several meters before coming to a stop at the mouth of a rocky tunnel that stretched deep within the mountain. Must be home, she thought wryly. Then she began to creep along the tunnel. Several times she had to step over the remains of what she could only assume were Raiders, judging by the white tattered robes that covered the skeletons. The carcasses of womp rats also lined the tunnel. Tahiri tried to ignore them as she snuck along.

Anakin was crouched in the center of a basically round room, the only light there filtered through small holes in the ceiling that were exposed to the surface of the mountain. As Tahiri's eyes adjusted, she saw that the lair was also littered with the skeletons of womp rats and some brown-robed remains. The dragon was rustling on the far side of the room. Now that he had Anakin, he didn't seem to be in too much of a rush to eat him. Must be saving him for later, Tahiri thought with deadly calm. All the fear that had initially coursed through her veins had drained away. In its place, she felt the strength of the Force surging through her. There was no way she was going to allow the krayt dragon to hurt her friend.

Anakin sensed Tahiri's presence. He raised his face and peered into the darkness. Slowly he rose to knees, then gained his feet. Tahiri stepped out of the shadows and moved to Anakin's side. The side of his academy jumpsuit was drenched in blood, and Tahiri stifled a cry. Anakin grasped her hand tightly, and for a brief moment their eyes met. The look they exchanged was one of calm and resolve. They would fight this beast together.

The krayt dragon turned and rose on its hind feet. A thin screech rolled out. Its dinner was being threatened, and that made the reptile angry. Very angry. Slowly the dragon advanced on the Jedi candidates. And in a flash it had snatched Anakin and pinned him beneath its clawed feet.

"My voice didn't work," Anakin groaned to

Tahiri. "So we've got to try something else." He stared into the razor teeth that lined the creature's jaws. "And soon, because its breath will kill me if its teeth don't first."

Tahiri stared desperately around the lair for a weapon. Her eyes stopped on a large boulder that jutted out on the far side of the room. Maybe I can distract him, she thought, and then we can try to run. Tahiri closed her eyes and focused on using the Force to pry the boulder loose. Nothing happened.

"Any ideas?" Anakin gasped as the dragon stared down at him with hungry eyes.

"Believe and you succeed," Tahiri murmured to herself as she continued concentrating on the rock. Moments later there was a thunderous crash.

TWELVE

The rancid breath of the reptile rolled over Anakin in hot waves. It opened its jaws wide, preparing to crush and consume him. Tahiri stood in the center of the dragon's lair, her eyes closed.

There was a thunderous crash behind the dragon, and clouds of dust and sand filled the room. The reptile whirled and raced toward the noise. It must think something is attacking from behind, Tahiri thought as she opened her eyes and watched.

Anakin leapt to his feet and raced to Tahiri's side.

"Run!" he cried as he tore toward the tunnel.

"No," Tahiri called after her friend. "The dragon is too fast—it'll just catch us and bring us back. We've got to stand and fight it."

"But it's too strong," Anakin exclaimed. "We can't."

The dust cleared, and Tahiri watched the dragon slither away from the boulder she'd dropped. The reptile turned back to its prisoners, crimson eyes flashing that it would not let them get away. She noticed several large rocks lining the ceiling of the cave, only a few meters in front of where the dragon now stood. "We have to trap it beneath those rocks," Tahiri murmured.

"Anakin, we've got to try to drop those boulders on it," Tahiri said as she pointed to the outcropping of rocks. Anakin nodded, and the Jedi candidates began to focus. There wasn't much time. Tahiri sensed that the dragon was about to dart forward. She repeated part of the Jedi Code to herself: *There is no try, only do.* And, as the words faded away, so did her fear and frustration.

Tahiri heard the boulders begin to move, a grating sound combined with dropping dust and pebbles. She opened her eyes and watched as the krayt dragon began to move forward. "Now, Anakin!" Tahiri cried. "Drop them now!" In a split second, five large boulders hurtled down through the air and landed with dull thuds on the krayt dragon's tail. The reptile roared with frustration as it tried to reach the Jedi candidates. Its tail was firmly pinned beneath the boulders.

"Now let's get out of here before the dragon gets those boulders off!" Anakin said.

On their way out, Tahiri grabbed several abandoned canteens of water. Whoever had brought them into the dragon's lair no longer needed them, and she and Anakin would need all the water they could find to cross the mesa region of the Wastes and the desert beyond, Tahiri thought.

It took the night of their fourth day and all of the fifth to cross the mesa. They slept for two hours each during the hottest part of the day, one keeping watch, then the other. Once, Tahiri spied a tribe of Raiders in the distance, but the group didn't seem to notice them.

By the evening of day five, Anakin and Tahiri reached the desert. They were almost out of water, now only taking small sips from the one battered green canteen they had left. Tahiri's lips were cracked from the dryness, and her pale skin was red and burned from the harsh suns. Anakin's gashes from the krayt dragon had stopped bleeding, but they had begun to fester, and infection had set in. He winced as he bent to put the water jug back in the pack.

"Does it hurt very badly?" Tahiri asked as she gently touched the side of his tattered jumpsuit.

Anakin smiled at his friend. "Not too bad," he replied. "It's not important. What matters is figuring out how we're going to find your tribe. We've crossed the Dune Sea and the Wastes, but we don't have enough water to survive much longer. And we only have two days left to fulfill the promise."

Tahiri stared at her friend. He looked terrible.

His skin was deep pink. His eyes were ringed with purple circles. The gashes on his side were infected. He needed medical attention and food. Something sparkled in the distance and caught Tahiri's eye. "Wait here," Tahiri called to her friend as she trotted off.

"Where are you going?" Anakin asked. But if Tahiri heard him, she didn't reply.

Ten minutes later Tahiri stood before the sparkling object she'd spied in the distance. It was a hubba gourd, a tough-skinned melon covered with tiny reflective crystals. She picked it up and returned to her friend.

"What is it?" Anakin asked when Tahiri tossed him the oblong melon.

"It's a kind of fruit," Tahiri explained. "Hard to digest, but it's food." Tahiri pulled her multitool out of her pocket and began to carve up the melon. She and Anakin ate slowly. When they were done, Tahiri took the hubba rinds and placed them over the gashes on Anakin's ribs.

"Raider medicine?" Anakin asked with a wry smile.

"Sliven taught me that the rind of the hubba gourd helps stop infections," Tahiri said. "Your cuts are already infected, but this might slow it down." Tahiri tore some material off the sleeves of Anakin's jumpsuit and bound the rinds to his rib cage.

Then she sat down to consider their options.

What we need is a bantha, Tahiri thought. That wasn't exactly right. What they needed was *her* bantha, Bangor. Bangor would be able to lead them back to the tribe.

"Which way?" Anakin asked, interrupting Tahiri's thoughts.

Tahiri scanned the horizon. Sand dunes everywhere and no sign of her tribe. They could be just over the next dune or a hundred kilometers from where they now stood.

"I've always felt a deep bond with Bangor," Tahiri said.

Anakin stared at his friend, wondering why she was talking about her bantha.

Tahiri continued, "I believe that banthas are more complicated than my people know. Bangor has always been able to sense my fears."

"A lot of creatures have the ability to sense fear," Anakin interrupted.

"It's not just that," Tahiri replied. "There were times in my life when I needed Bangor—if I was sad or lonely, he always came to me. It was as if he heard me calling him for comfort."

"Are you saying what I think you're saying?" Anakin asked.

"Yes," Tahiri said, meeting his eyes. "I'm going to try to call Bangor to us. We're almost out of food and water, and we're definitely out of strength," she added gravely. "If we don't get to the tribe soon, we'll die out here."

THIRTEEN

Anakin stared at the horizon. The suns were beginning to drop, and soon night would come. Their sixth night. They had only one more day to find the tribe. If they failed, for whatever reason, Sliven would be put to death. "Tahiri, it's not working," Anakin said softly almost two hours later.

Tahiri didn't reply.

"We should start walking again," Anakin gently suggested. He stared at his friend. The strips of cloth she'd torn from the bottom of her jumpsuit and used to cover her head were crusted with sweat and sand. Hollow green eyes stared up at him. But he didn't have an answer.

Suddenly Tahiri's listless eyes flashed. "Let me try to call Bangor again," Tahiri said. "You try too, Anakin," she instructed. "Maybe he'll hear our voices calling if we work together."

Anakin nodded. He didn't have the heart to deny Tahiri's request. Together they reached over the rolling dunes with their voices and called the bantha with the Force. They stood back to back, calling Bangor over and over again. Finally, they sat down in the sands, leaning against each other for support.

"Maybe we should sleep and then try again in a bit," Tahiri murmured, her eyes already closed.

Anakin huddled next to Tahiri as the night blanketed them with its cold threads. His last thought before sleep carried him away was that when he awoke it would be day seven.

"Quit it," Tahiri mumbled as a dry nose nudged her. Then her eyes shot open. Bangor stood above her, his brown eyes staring kindly down at his friend. From his neck dangled a thick rope that was frayed at the end. The bantha had broken his line to come to their rescue. Tahiri struggled up and hugged the bantha as he snuggled his head against her shoulder. "Thank you, Bangor," she said softly. "Anakin, wake up and tell me if I'm still dreaming!" Tahiri cried to her friend.

"You're not dreaming!" Anakin croaked happily when he saw Bangor. Moments later the two Jedi candidates were on the bantha's back.

"Please take us to the tribe, Bangor," Tahiri said. The bantha began to lope across the sands. Anakin and Tahiri said little during the journey.

Both were thinking about what fulfilling the promise meant. They had gained strength in the Force, and had learned that working together produced more powerful results than they had dreamed possible.

Bangor began to slow. "Do you need some rest?" Tahiri asked the bantha. They had been loping across the desert for almost five hours. It was early evening, and Bangor had begun to weary. Now he quietly walked up a sand dune, coming to a rest only when he reached its crest.

"Is he all right?" Anakin asked Tahiri. But before she could answer, he saw why the bantha had stopped. Below them was Tahiri's tribe. Anakin could hear Vexa's words ringing above those of the rest of the Raiders. The tribe stood behind her. They appeared to be having some kind of meeting. Sliven stood apart from the Raiders. Only Tionne was by his side. "What's Vexa saying?" Anakin whispered to Tahiri as they slid off Bangor and hid behind the dune.

"She's asking the tribe to declare us dead," Tahiri began to translate. "She says that when the suns set, seven days will have passed and we will have failed to return." Sliven's deep bark interrupted Vexa. "Sliven says that we still have two hours. He asks the tribe to wait," Tahiri explained. Vexa began to grunt and bark angrily. She raised her gaderffii toward Sliven. "She says Sliven is weak, and it is time he left the tribe forever." Tahiri rose and walked to the top of the dune. Anakin followed his friend.

"Stop," Tahiri barked. All eyes turned to the crest of the dune. Vexa's disappointed cry couldn't be mistaken. Tahiri, Anakin, and Bangor made their way down the dune. Tahiri walked up to Vexa. "There is no honor in your actions," she said. Then she turned to the rest of the tribe. "We have returned before the suns set on the seventh day. Sliven is still your leader." The tribe members moved from Vexa to stand behind Sliven.

A Raider brought two water jugs over to Anakin and Tahiri. Tahiri cupped some water in her hands and held them out to Bangor. The bantha drank deeply as Tahiri buried her face in the creature's thick fur. "Thank you," she whispered. Bangor nuzzled against Tahiri, then moved back to the rest of the herd. After Anakin and Tahiri drank, Tahiri walked over to Sliven.

Tionne joined Anakin, her worried eyes scanning his wounds. There would be time to talk about what had happened later, Tionne thought. For now, it was enough that Anakin and Tahiri were alive. Together Anakin and Tionne watched as Tahiri spoke softly to Sliven.

"He said that he's glad in his heart that I survived," Tahiri explained when she returned. "He hopes that all my worry about who I am has ended. In his mind, I'm a Raider. And he believes I should stay with my tribe."

"And what do you believe?" Anakin asked. His heart skipped a beat. If Tahiri stayed on Tatooine, he would lose his best friend, and alone he might not be able to break the curse of the golden globe. Still, he wouldn't try to sway her decision. She had to do what was right for her.

"I'm glad we succeeded," Tahiri softly began. "I now understand that I was never a Tusken Raider. The skills we both used to survive weren't the skills of a Raider. We used the Force. And now I know that I'm meant to attend the academy. To grow strong, and to use that strength to break the curse of the golden globe, and one day become a Jedi Knight."

"What about Sliven? Won't you miss him?" Anakin asked.

"That's the hardest part," Tahiri said sadly. "I love Sliven, but I know that I belong at the Jedi academy, not with the Sand People."

"Then let us leave here," Tionne said.

"I've got to do one last thing," Tahiri said quietly. Anakin watched as his friend walked back to Sliven and told him her decision. The Raider nodded once, then reached inside his robes. He held out a roughly shaped pendant. In its center was his thumbprint. Tahiri unclasped the chain from her neck and threaded the gift through it. When she reclasped her chain, two sand-colored pendants hung from it. On them were the prints of her parents—all three of them.

"You will always be a part of me," Tahiri said softly to Sliven. "In my heart, you're my father. Please take care of Bangor for me—he's yours, just like I'm yours," she whispered, swallowing a lump in her throat. Tahiri moved forward and wrapped her arms around Sliven's waist. The Raider hugged his daughter back.

FOURTEEN

Anakin awoke with his side on fire—the gashes from the krayt dragon were now infected stripes of oozing yellow pus. Tionne sat by his side, placing a cold compress to his forehead and medicating his cuts. Old Peckhum clucked and worried as he guided the *Lightning Rod* back to Yavin 4. Anakin knew the old supply courier had been upset by his and Tahiri's appearance when they'd returned to his ship from the desert. "We're both fine," Anakin had reassured him. But he allowed Peckhum to help him into the supply ship, wincing in pain as he was lowered onto a sleeping pad. Tahiri and Tionne sat beside him the entire return trip. Anakin drifted in and out of consciousness, burning with fever.

So much has happened, Anakin thought as the ship sped through the atmosphere. Only a week ago, I wondered if Tahiri and I were ready to attempt to enter the golden globe and free the Massassi children. Now I know that we're strong enough. . . . Together we've used the Force to escape a giant tentacled creature, befriended Jawas with help from the Force, and defeated a krayt dragon. Anakin's thoughts swirled with dizziness, fever, and fatigue. He did not even hear Peckhum's voice signaling that they would soon land on Yavin 4.

Luke Skywalker waited for the *Lightning Rod*'s cargo bay to open. Slowly the massive jaws of the bay yawned wide, revealing Luke's nephew and Tahiri. Luke was pleased to see that the girl had returned. She belonged at the Jedi academy. He moved forward to greet the Jedi candidates. "Welcome home—" Master Luke began. But his words caught in his throat as he stared at his students.

Anakin struggled to stand and walk down the cargo bay's ramp. Old Peckhum held one of his arms tightly, steadying him as he walked. Anakin took several tottering steps, then fell forward. Luke anticipated his nephew's collapse, and caught the boy in his arms. Gently he lowered Anakin to the ground. Anakin's academy jumpsuit was shredded on one side, revealing five gashes. There were dark circles under his eyes, and bruises were visible on his neck and hands. Tahiri knelt by her friend. The girl did not look much better, Luke thought in dismay. Spots of dried blood lined her jumpsuit in a pattern that looked like jaw marks. She, too, looked tired and hungry. Luke's eyes met Tionne's for a brief moment. From her look of torment, he knew she'd tried her best to protect the children.

"Hi, Uncle Luke," Anakin said with a small voice.

"What happened?" Luke asked in a voice full of worry.

"The Tusken Raiders had a little more in mind for me than just deciding whether or not to remain with the tribe," Tahiri replied.

"We'll talk later," Luke said quietly to Tionne. "Right now, you are both going to the medical droid." With that, he swept his nephew up in his arms and strode toward the turbolift, with Tahiri trailing.

Anakin awoke. He was lying in his room, a medical droid hovering in the corner, his uncle seated beside his bed. Anakin stared down at his ribs. They were bandaged in soft, white gauze.

"You're awake," Luke Skywalker said. Anakin smiled. "And you can smile; that's good," Luke said softly. His pale blue eyes reflected his concern.

"Is Tahiri all right?" Anakin asked.

"Yes," Luke replied gravely. "And she told me what happened. If I'd known what the Raiders had in mind, I would never have allowed either of you to go to Tatooine. Sliven gave his word that neither of you would be harmed. . . ." Luke's voice trailed off.

"His word was worth more than you know," Anakin said in Sliven's defense. "Tahiri chose to fulfill Sliven's promise—he didn't force her," Anakin added. Anakin saw a look of doubt shadow his uncle's face. "It was something she had to do," he tried to explain. "I don't think she could have returned to the academy if she hadn't . . . and I couldn't let her go alone."

"Your mother wanted me to send you home," Master Luke said, changing the subject. "Han and I persuaded her to let you stay at the academy. You're bruised, you haven't had enough water, and those gashes were infected," Luke said, pointing to Anakin's ribs, "but there wasn't any serious damage."

"How long have I been sleeping?" Anakin asked.

"Two days," his uncle replied. Anakin tried to sit up, and fell back as a sickening wave of dizziness washed over him. "It's going to take a few more days before you're ready to get up," Luke said gently.

Anakin settled back against his pillows. He didn't like the idea of waiting. The time to break the curse was already thousands of years overdue. But a day or two more wouldn't matter. And

Anakin knew that he'd need all his strength to enter the globe and free the children. He resolved to get well quickly.

Luke Skywalker studied the intensity of Anakin's ice blue eyes. He understood all too well that his nephew and Tahiri were tied together by more than their bond of friendship. They were true Jedi, and someday they would become powerful Jedi Knights. From what Tahiri had told him of their adventures on Tatooine, they were already well on their way. But, he worried that these two Jedi candidates were in the habit of rushing headlong into dangerous situations. What if they found themselves in one they weren't ready for?

"Regardless of whether or not Tahiri needed to learn her history, it was foolhardy to risk your lives in the deserts of Tatooine," Luke Skywalker said softly. He watched Anakin's face fall, and couldn't continue his attempt to rein in his nephew. "Still, you used your minds and the Force well." So well, Luke thought in amazement, that he could hardly fathom the strength still to be developed in the candidates. Anakin's face beamed up at his uncle. "Now get well, or Leia will never forgive me," Luke instructed.

Luke Skywalker sat beside his nephew as he slept. He wondered if the strange feeling of untold danger he'd sensed before sending the children to

Tatooine had been a premonition of the promise Tahiri had chosen to keep. Luke closed his eyes and breathed a sigh of relief. At least the children were safe.

FIFTEEN

He was in the depths of the Palace of the Woolamander. The damp, rotting smell of evil flowed in invisible currents along the crumbling stones. He moved toward the small room, bathed by a sickly sweet smell that oozed around his head, filled his ears, and attempted to enter his mouth. Still, he was calm. He knew what had to be done.

When he reached the room, he walked toward the crystal sphere. The swirling golden sands cast a yellow gleam along his extended arm. He opened his hand and placed his right palm on the surface of the globe. A jolt of pain began at his fingertips and traveled the length of his arm in a white-hot torrent. And then the voices began.

"You will fail," they called from the darkness. "You will be swallowed by the dark side. Swallowed into the belly of evil, where you will live forever, tortured and twisting in agony. It doesn't have to be that way, boy," a single voice said from the darkness. He recognized it. It was the evil follower of Exar Kun. The being that had haunted his dreams. "Join us now, and the glory of the dark side will be yours. You already belong to us," the figure hissed. "You just don't know it yet."

He let the voice fall from him, until it lay in an oily black pool at his feet. Then he extended his other palm to the globe, and let the now familiar pain cascade through his left arm. This time it did not stop at his shoulder. Instead, it continued to course through his body, wrapping his torso in a vice grip of pain. "I am coming," Anakin called out to the children inside the globe through clenched teeth. "I am coming, and nothing can stop me."

"Anakin?" Tahiri called from the side of his sleeping pad. "Anakin? Are you all right?"

Slowly, Anakin woke. He stared up into the worried eyes of his friend. She looked better. There were still traces of bluish rings beneath her eyes, and her sunburned face was beginning to peel, but the light was back in her emerald green eyes.

"Are you all right?" Tahiri bubbled. Without waiting for an answer, she continued. "I was so worried. I mean I was pretty sick too, but Master Luke said that you had an infection and a fever. Do you still have one—a fever, I mean?"

Anakin grinned. He hadn't heard Tahiri's customary chatter since they'd begun their adventure on Tatooine. It was nice to see that she was back to normal.

"Bantha got your tongue?" Tahiri teased.

"As usual, I was just waiting for the chance to get a word in edgewise," Anakin replied. Slowly, he sat up. He felt better, much better. He moved toward the open window and stared out into the jungle. "Are you ready, Tahiri?" he finally asked.

"Yes," Tahiri replied from behind him. "Are you?"

Anakin nodded.

"Are you certain you are strong enough?" a deep, raspy voice called from the corner of the room. It was Ikrit. The Jedi Master, his white fur and the stones of the Great Temple strangely blending, scurried from the corner and leapt onto the window ledge. "After all," he rasped, "this is only one battle of good versus evil. There will be others, if you are not up to the fight."

Anakin stared into Ikrit's round, brown eyes. Eyes that told nothing. Eyes that waited passively for their decision. "There are some battles that have to be fought, regardless of the risks or odds. Light versus dark, good versus evil. Those battles can't be ignored," Anakin said softly.

"What if we're not strong enough?" Tahiri asked with uneasy concern.

"I believe that we are," Anakin replied. "If we ignore the workings of the dark side of the Force, then we allow evil to triumph. And if that happens, it won't just mean the lives of the children trapped within the globe—it will cast a shadow of darkness on our own lives."

Tahiri nodded. "Evil can't be ignored," she agreed. "Regardless of the risks."

"Then may the Force be with you," Master Ikrit rasped. With that, he scurried out the window, made his way down the pyramid-shaped wall of the Great Temple, and disappeared into the jungles of Yavin 4.

"I guess Master Ikrit won't be coming with us," Tahiri said.

"We're on our own," Anakin added softly. "Whatever happens, we're on our own."

Anakin turned back to the jungles and let the sweet scent fill him. He thought about his dream, and what it meant. It was the second time he had dreamed about the follower of Exar Kun. The second time he'd defeated Kun's follower by using the Force to control his inner self and make the evil figure's threats useless. Anakin only hoped he'd be able to do the same in the Palace of the Woolamander. There was no doubt in his mind that the spirits of Kun's evil followers would be there for real, attempting to stop them from breaking the curse and freeing the globe's children, trying to turn Tahiri and him to the dark side.

And what about entering the globe? Anakin wondered. Had his dream been right? Was it a matter of enduring the pain of the powerful field until it lost its strength and let Anakin inside the sphere? Anakin turned to Tahiri to tell her about his dream, and to try to figure out how they were going to lead the Massassi children to freedom. They were in this together, and they would succeed together, or never leave the palace alive.

SIXTEEN

They knew the way. Hidden by darkness, Tahiri and Anakin raced through the jungles of Yavin 4. The first time they'd snuck out of the Great Temple to raft the river, they hadn't known where they were going. This time, they were guided by their memories and their convictions. They felt the weight of the Palace of the Woolamander before it loomed above them, a crumbling site of darkness and buried evil. Neither spoke as they entered an opening that had once been a majestic portal, or when they saw the familiar Massassi symbols carved along the walls of the palace. The time for talk or solving riddles was long past. The time for action was at hand.

Anakin flashed his light beam toward a broken wall that hid the crumbling stairway they'd descended a month before. Several large woolamanders scurried out of the hole and into the

103

darkness. Neither Anakin nor Tahiri jumped in surprise. There were bigger things to be afraid of.

"Ready?" Anakin asked Tahiri. She moved forward and climbed through a hole in the crumbling wall. Anakin followed. Hand in hand, they began to descend the spiral stairway.

The voices began. "Go back," they called as the Jedi candidates climbed down the stairs. "This is a dark place; you are not welcome here," they rumbled.

"We've been here, and heard that before," Tahiri shot into the darkness. "It didn't work the first time, so just give it a rest."

"Orphan child, you cannot break the curse," a voice said from the darkness.

"Now that's new," Tahiri murmured under her breath. She and Anakin continued to descend.

"Orphan child, you are a sister of the darkness," the voice hissed to Tahiri. "We are your family; your home is with us. Leave the boy. He is not one of us. He doesn't care about you."

Anakin recognized the voice from his dreams. He felt Tahiri's anger growing. "Tahiri, that's what they want," he whispered urgently. "They want you to strike out against them, to use the Force in aggression. Remember, a Jedi never acts from anger, hatred, or aggression."

"Your mother, Cassa, was one of us. So was your father, Tryst," the voice lied. "Join them and finally understand who you really are."

"I am Tahiri Veila, daughter of Cassa and Tryst," Tahiri began softly as she and Anakin continued to descend. "I'm Tahiri, chosen daughter of Sliven of the Tusken Raiders. My path is one of light. I am a Jedi candidate."

Anakin felt Tahiri's anger ebbing. Her hand, which had moments before clung tightly to his, relaxed.

"Boy," a familiar voice called from the gloom. "You aren't like your little friend. You are part of the history of the dark side. Your grandfather, Anakin Skywalker, served Emperor Palpatine well. The seed of evil is planted within you. It is your birthright—don't fight it," the voice insisted.

Anakin felt the words slither around his body like snakes. All the fear he had about who he was, and the burden of carrying the name "Anakin," fought to rise to the surface. He felt an overwhelming need to strike out against the evil follower of Kun. But instead, he laughed. It was a small laugh at first, but it grew stronger as Tahiri joined in. And the louder the Jedi students laughed, the weaker the voice became, until it went out, like a flame before a hearty wind.

Anakin and Tahiri reached the base of the stairs and walked toward the doorway they'd entered before to discover the globe. But nothing could have prepared them for what they saw and heard. Nothing.

The children were crying. Anakin could hear

their strangled sobs the moment he stepped inside the room. Countless ghostlike hands were pressed against the inside of the globe, torn away by the madly swirling sands, only to reappear moments later in silent pleas for help. "The followers of Exar Kun are trying to destroy the children before we can free them," Anakin said in horror.

Tahiri ran toward the globe before Anakin could stop her, and struck it with her fists. The field repelled her efforts, tossing her through the air. Her body somersaulted once, then struck the stone wall. Anakin raced over to his friend, who lay crumpled on the floor. He helped her to sit up, and watched as she shook her head slowly from side to side to clear it from the blow.

Tahiri looked up at Anakin with agonized green eyes. "They're dying in there!" she cried. "Anakin, we've got to do something!"

SEVENTEEN

The pain that extended from the globe through Anakin's right palm and across his chest was sheer agony. He fought to remain standing, to absorb the field as it coursed through his body like white lightning, to make it harmless. His legs buckled from the torture, and he fell to his knees. Tahiri leapt forward and tore her friend from the field's stranglehold. They both fell back, Anakin breathing in rattled gasps as the pain slowly subsided.

"There's got to be another way!" Tahiri said. "What if we both focus on using the Force to weaken the field," Tahiri thought out loud. "Anakin, you did it when you weakened the reel on Yavin 8," she continued. "Once the field is weak enough, we can both enter the globe and find the children."

"You're right, Tahiri," Anakin replied, rising to

his feet. "But I don't think we should go inside together. We have no idea what it's like inside the globe. If one of us fails, the other needs to be able to help, or to go get help if there's no other choice." Tahiri nodded. "I want to go in first," Anakin said softly. The hard glint in his eyes told Tahiri there could be no arguing.

Anakin moved toward the globe. Tahiri stood by his side. There were no more words. Both knew what had to be done. They closed their eyes and reached out to the field with the Force. The field sparked and flared as their minds tried to weaken it. Anakin felt sweat roll down his forehead. His back cramped with effort. And, just when he almost began to lose hope, he felt a tiny weakening in the field. "It's working," Anakin said through clenched teeth. Tahiri squeezed his hand. She could feel it, too.

Moments later, the field's strength flickered, then faded to a soft buzz in Anakin's mind. Without pausing, he reached toward the smooth sphere. He felt his hands pass through the crystal, felt the stinging of the golden sands on his flesh. It's now or never, Anakin thought. He plunged forward, his body entering the globe, then disappearing from view in the swirling sands. He felt a sharp bolt of pain as his right foot slid inside the sphere. The field had regained its power.

It's like swimming through sand, Anakin

thought as he fought his way through the whirl-
pool of golden particles. The sands stung and
blinded him, and he covered his nose and mouth
with the sleeve of his jumpsuit so that he could
breathe. Then he began to search for the children.

Strange, Anakin thought; from the outside, the
globe is no more than four meters across, but inside it's huge. Anakin blindly struggled to find his
way through the globe. His body was tossed and
tumbled in the mad whirls of sand until he no
longer knew up from down. He cried out to the
children, but there was no answer.

And then there they were, crowding around
him, their small hands reaching out, grasping the
folds of his jumpsuit, touching his face, his hair.
There were so many of them, Anakin wondered
how he could lead them all out of the globe. "Grab
hands!" he called out. "All of you, grab hands."
They understood, and he felt two small hands
slide into his. Anakin battled through the storm
as the sands filled his nose and mouth and threatened to choke him. He had to lead them to the
edge of the crystal, through the field, he thought,
his legs struggling as the sands thickened.

"Help me, Tahiri!" Anakin cried into the deaf-
ening churn and the sea of frightened cries. He
fell, and the sands tossed him in a dizzying rush.

EIGHTEEN

"Anakin, where are you!" Tahiri screamed as her friend's fear reached out from the globe and filled her senses. There was no answer. "This is not the way it's going to end!" she cried into the darkness.

"Anakin!" Tahiri called over and over with her voice and the Force. A glimpse of his orange jumpsuit appeared, then disappeared as the sands violently whirled. "Anakin, I'm here!" Tahiri cried.

Anakin heard Tahiri's voice through the sands, and struggled toward it, his hands still firmly clenching the small hands of two Massassi children. He pressed forward, toward Tahiri's cries, until he ran headlong into the crystal. Anakin pressed the backs of his hands against the globe, letting the pain of the field course down his arms until he was certain that Tahiri had seen him.

111

Then he focused on the field, once again using the Force to weaken it. He sensed Tahiri joining her strength with his.

Sands wrapped around Anakin's legs like the tentacles of the creature on Tatooine and tried to draw him back into the center of the globe. Anakin fought to keep his footing, to concentrate on weakening the field. But he was growing tired, and the current was close to toppling him and breaking his resolve. Before him the field's strength began to flicker and falter. There was no more time to wait. Anakin reached forward, ignoring the ripples of pain that ran down his arms and made him cry out. He thrust his fists through the field, feeling the dank air of the chamber beyond. Anakin forged ahead, pushing through the field with the last of his strength, absorbing its weakened power in dull aches and hot flashes.

Suddenly he was through, his hands drawing the children behind him in a steady stream. Anakin forced his mind back to the field, joining Tahiri in a last effort to weaken its power as the children streamed from the globe, hand in hand. Minutes later it was over, the last child emerging from the globe's cursed grasp. Anakin sank to the stone floor.

"You're free," Tahiri said softly to the countless children who crowded the chamber. Their small, spiritlike forms were almost transparent. Cloaked in white robes outlined in shimmering blue, they stood silently before the Jedi candidates. "Do you think they understand?" Tahiri asked as she sat down beside Anakin.

"They understand," Anakin answered, sensing the children's growing wonderment and joy. One of them walked toward the Jedi candidates. He reached out a small hand and gently touched both of their faces. Anakin felt the brush of a feather across his cheek at the touch. Then the Massassi child bowed and moved back to the other children. Slowly they all began to fade from sight, until the last glimmering blue outline disappeared. They had finally returned to their people.

The curse was broken; the children were freed from their imprisonment. "Do you feel it?" Anakin asked Tahiri.

Tahiri nodded. "Peace to all," she replied softly.

As Tahiri and Anakin moved to leave the chamber, they heard a sharp sound behind them, and whirled. The golden globe was cracking, its surface lined with running veins of white. Then, in an instant, the sphere broke into a thousand shards of crystal, and the golden glitter which had once filled it spilled out into the chamber, now just lifeless yellow sand.

Anakin and Tahiri left the Palace of the Woolamander. Their eyes quickly adjusted from the gloom to the soft morning light of the jungle. And to the figure of Jedi Master Luke Skywalker as he stood on the crumbling stone steps of the palace, Master Ikrit by his side.

Luke Skywalker studied Anakin and Tahiri. His face conveyed relief at seeing the two Jedi candidates safe. "The curse is broken?" Luke asked softly.

"Yes," Anakin answered his uncle.

"You have both done well," Ikrit rasped, his big brown eyes gleaming in pride at Tahiri and Anakin.

"You know everything?" Anakin asked his uncle, gesturing toward Ikrit.

Luke Skywalker nodded. He wrapped his arms around Anakin's and Tahiri's shoulders. "I am very proud," Luke said, his eyes meeting theirs.

Slowly the group walked back toward the Jedi academy. For the first time in a long time, Anakin and Tahiri were not heading toward danger, but simply toward the future—adventure, the Force, and their ultimate goal: to become Jedi Knights.

Follow the further adventures
of the Junior Jedi Knights in
ANAKIN'S QUEST,
written by Rebecca Moesta,
co-author of *The New York Times* bestselling
YOUNG JEDI KNIGHTS.
Coming in July,
from Boulevard Books.

Anakin has been having terrible dreams of a
secret cave on the swamp planet Dagobeh. Together with Tahiri, R2-D2 and the Jedi Master
Ikrit, he travels there to face whatever danger
lurks inside.